ED AND THE
WITCHBLOOD

Andrew Fusek Peters & Stephen Player

Hodder
Children's
Books

Text copyright ©2003 Andrew Fusek Peters
Illustrations copyright ©2003 Stephen Player

First published in Great Britain in 2003
by Hodder Children's Books.
This paperback edition published in 2004

3 5 7 9 10 8 6 4 2

Designer: Jane Hawkins
Consultant: Wendy Cooling

A Catalogue record for this book is available from the
British Library.

ISBN 0 340 86557 1

Printed and bound at Clays Ltd, St Ives plc

The paper used in this book is a natural recyclable product
made from wood grown in sustainable forests. The hardcover
board is recycled.

Hodder Children's Books
A division of Hodder Headline Limited
338 Euston Road, London NW1 3BH

ED AND THE WITCHBLOOD

Andrew Fusek Peters is a much praised poet and storyteller working in schools around the UK. He also works extensively in television. With his wife Polly Peters, he is the author of the highly successful **Poems With Attitude** and its successor **Poems With Attitude: Uncensored.**

The Guardian said of **Poems With Attitude**: 'Bursting with the raw emotion and hormone-fuelled experimentation of youth ... It is rare and welcome to find a collection that speaks so directly to teenagers.'

For more information about Andrew, visit his web site at www.tallpoet.com

Stephen Player is a highly experienced illustrator whose work includes illustrations for books by Clive Barker and Terry Pratchett as well as numerous childre Born in Hertfordshire, he recently moved f San Francisco. For more information about his web site at www.playergallery.com

Dedications:

To Maurice, with many thanks for the concept and in memory of Bruce Barr, the greatest poetry player in Shropshire – AP

For Dave – SP

Andrew Fusek Peters acknowledges the support of a Creative Ambition Award from Arts Council England – West Midlands in writing this book.

Thread of the witch is
Woven with care,
Fire, earth, water, air;
Hail the sky's long lost daughter,
Air, earth, fire, water;
Life dies, a ghost gives birth,
Water, air, fire, earth;
I stamp and breathe a roaring choir,
Earth, air, water, fire:
Bind these elements one by one,
Adding time 'til times are done,
But the sixth, the final prize?
How to meet the enemy's eyes?
Stronger than the singing sword,
This shall have them overawed.

Somehow I know I am going to love this school.

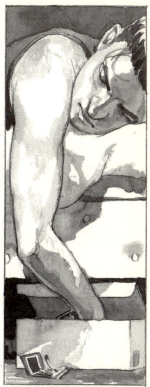

Not like it was though...

This bloody clutch! I thought you were supposed to be building this car, Edric!

Give me a chance, Dad.

Anyhow, you've just missed out the thrust bearing.

My son, the automotive world is awaiting you!

Yeah, right Mum!

What's with the macho-man medallion thing? You're always fiddling with it, Dad.

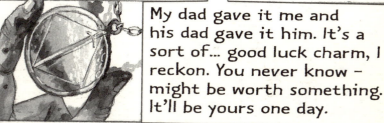

My dad gave it me and his dad gave it him. It's a sort of... good luck charm, I reckon. You never know – might be worth something. It'll be yours one day.

Come on you two, dinner's up. Bow before the Queen of Cookery!

Next day

I just don't get it. One minute she's here and next, she's gone. Like some weird, bloody vanishing act. And only took the clothes she stood up in and the earrings she wore.

Even though we're in the middle of London, this house seems to attract animals and birds... The night Mum disappeared, I heard a whole flock of starlings going mad on the rooftop.

This stupid bloody letter. What did we do wrong? I miss her. I don't get it.

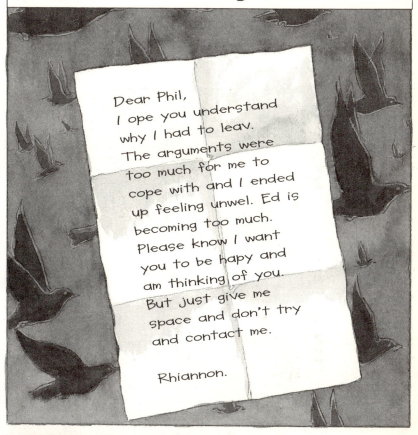

Haven't heard a thing from Mum. This is unbelievable. Dad is suggesting, or rather Luci is pressuring him, that I might be happier living with Grandad in Shropshire. He seems to have changed. It's all happening too fast.....

Mum gone and now this fiend who seems to have stolen my Dad.

It makes me sick to think of them having it away in my Mum's bed.

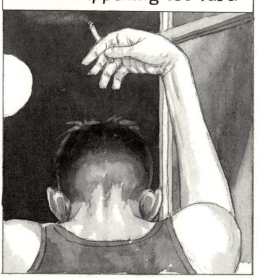

It's all happening too fast.

I miss her too, you know. Nothing. Not a word from my little girl...

...She had some gift with animals. I once saw a buzzard land on her outstretched arm and sit there while she stroked it's proud head. Amazing! Oh well.

Talisman, talisman,
Where have you been?
Ah, we have been
To see the old king.
So many sleeping
under the ground.
Time and season
Twisting round.
Who will wake them?
Who the man
To wield the power
of Talisman?

Anyhow, I saw what happened to you yesterday. Mitch is a tosser, but a very big tosser. Just give him the money.

Speak of the devil.

Later

You told me a tale. But that was a true one. Now, I'm going to tell you a tale about a different kind of bully.

Oh please, Grandad. I'm fifteen years old. Bit past all that!

Long ago, there was a famine
in the countryside round Stapely Hill.
This was hard country, easy to get
lost in during winter.

It was also the time
of the Fair Folk, what we call the
Fairies. One of them summoned a white
cow and put her in the stone circle. Each
villager could take a single bucket of milk
and the supply would never run dry.
Hunger vanished, and the people laid
baskets of whinberries on the hills
as thanks.

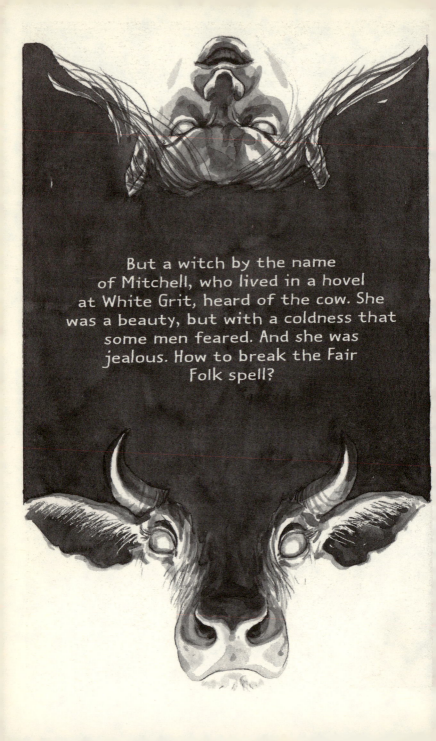

But a witch by the name
of Mitchell, who lived in a hovel
at White Grit, heard of the cow. She
was a beauty, but with a coldness that
some men feared. And she was
jealous. How to break the Fair
Folk spell?

With a wand and
what was once called a
riddle, a simple sieve,
instead of a bucket. Off she
went on a full moon night to
milk the cow dry. The spell
was broke and Mitchell
danced with glee.

The villagers found her
out. They rose up in fury. Came
with burning torches to her hovel.
Pushed her to the stone circle.
Made her dig a grave and buried
her alive in the middle.

Some said she left a baby
son, wailing in the night. That
was then and this is now. She can
find no rest 'til she undoes
what was done.

To this day the stone circle is known as Mitchell's Fold. A few years back, a farmer grew annoyed at the stones on his track.

He moved one out of the way.

No-one knows what happened, but the
tractor overturned. He bled to death.

Next day

My grandson has suffered enough, losing his mum. And now I hear he is a victim of a lunch-money extortion racket!

I assure you... we have no such... will look into it.

You'll do more than look into it, unless you want me to ring the local paper and tell them what sort of school you are running!

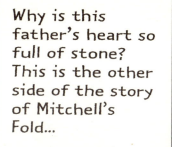

Why is this father's heart so full of stone? This is the other side of the story of Mitchell's Fold...

Cold. Cold, so cold, my old bones ache,
Only the crow for company.
The wind has skinned and soured me,
Burglar of all my beauty.
And I seethe like some lead-infected spring,
Metal in the dark soul of Mitchell.
And there's a reason, yes lovelies, a reason
For that little riddling trick with the sieve...

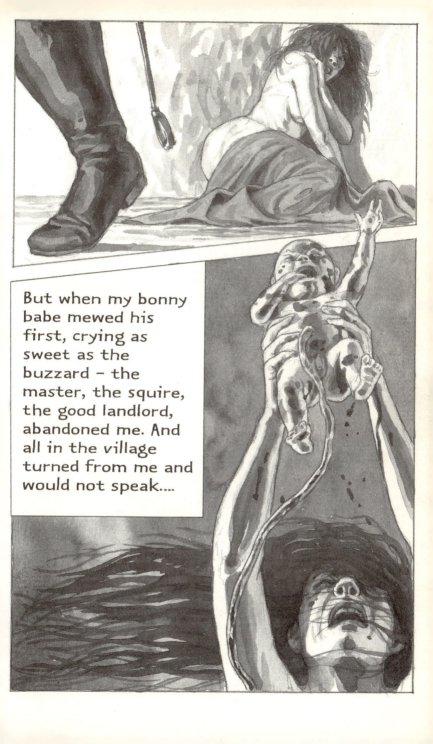

But when my bonny babe mewed his first, crying as sweet as the buzzard – the master, the squire, the good landlord, abandoned me. And all in the village turned from me and would not speak....

Today we will look at the pre-Cambrian rocks of South Shropshire, particularly the Quartzite out-crops of the Stiperstones.

The whole area is riddled with ancient Roman lead mines. Somewhere in there, Edric the Wild is fast asleep, waiting to wake and save the world. No, forget that. Edric is still asleep, aren't you boy?

No sir. Sorry sir. What?

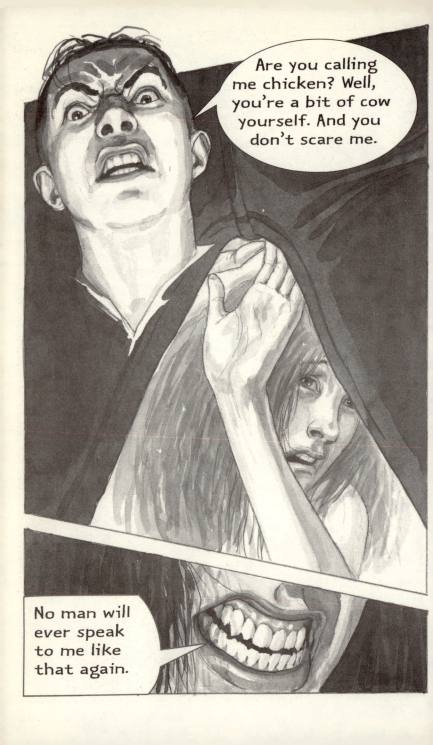

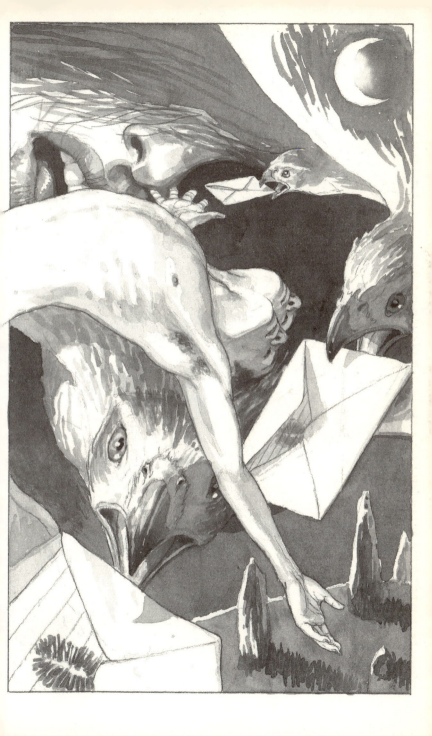

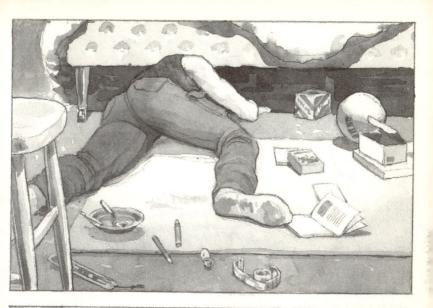

That dream.
The buzzard told me.
Dad never even noticed
I'd taken it. Too busy
with his new flame Luci.

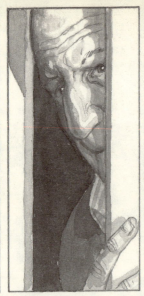

Aren't those your mum's?

Err... No. My mate Zack has got really peculiar taste in jewellery.

Listen, Shrewsbury are in the play-offs... against Luton.

You're out there somewhere Mum. I understood the letter, but what help can I give? Am I going mad – seeing witches, following buzzards and now talking to thin air? I'm stuck in this strange town in the middle of nowhere with a gang that make my life wonderfully miserable. Grandad is great, but I don't think he understands. I miss you so much. Yeah, I know I've gotta give up the fags – I can sense your wagging finger. See you.
See you soon.

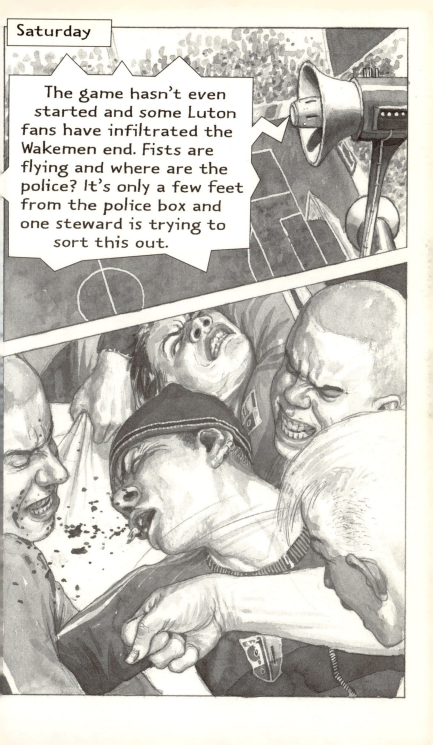

Oh well, just like school. In fact, it is school! I knew Mitch Craven and his thugs would be in there somewhere.

Is he the boy who...?

Yes.

Fists are not the only way to win, Ed. That lot should be ashamed of themselves.

Luton on the attack. Throw in. To Dickens, very comfortable with the ball. Sizes his options. To Ian Fleming, who nearly loses it, shaken, but not stirred. To Shelley. Now. Oh, monster! Shelley drives it and young Plath from Shrewsbury knocks it back to Yeats too hard. Oh! My word. It's an own goal!

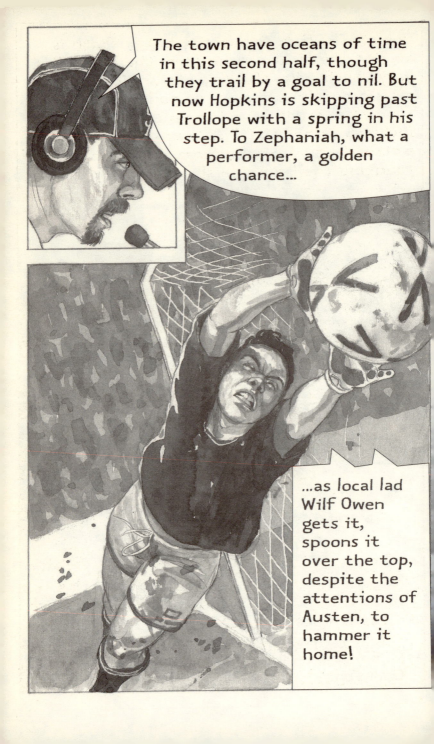

One all. The Hatters are not happy. Plath is leaving the field, and up from the bench it's Dafyd Ap-Gwylm, the Welsh lover. Hopefully he can produce the goods. The police have formed a cordon round the pitch to stop an invasion at the end. But that hasn't stopped a streaker jumping on from the riverside and taunting the Luton fans!

Tactics.... Well, maybe I can just think my way out of this bloody situation with our friendly local thuggery.

In fact, I feel an idea coming on. Time to pay another visit to a **very old** friend...

That night

In her circle now she stays,
Through the cold immortal days.
For our hunger, pay the price,
Her blood is frozen like the ice.

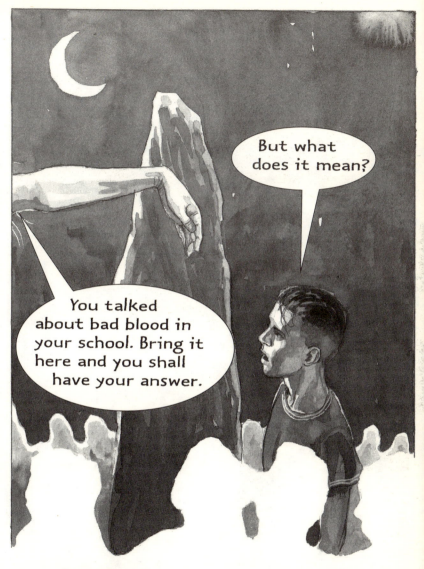

But if one comes and if he should
Let spill a pint of blood that's good
And mix it quickly with the bad,
Then her freedom shall be had.

Midsummer evening

I worked it out. Grandad told me the story, but there's more to it. He's yours – way down the line! When you were buried alive, you had a son, abandoned.

My bonny baby boy. Oh, he's gone. He's gone.

He had a son and his son had a son. They were all sons of Mitchell, cursed with hate and fear through too many generations. Mitch is the last in the line. He's your blood. Bad blood, good blood, mixed together. The curse is broken. You're free.

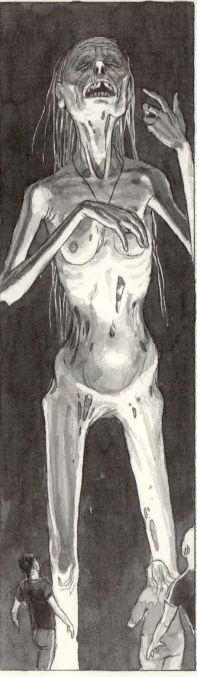

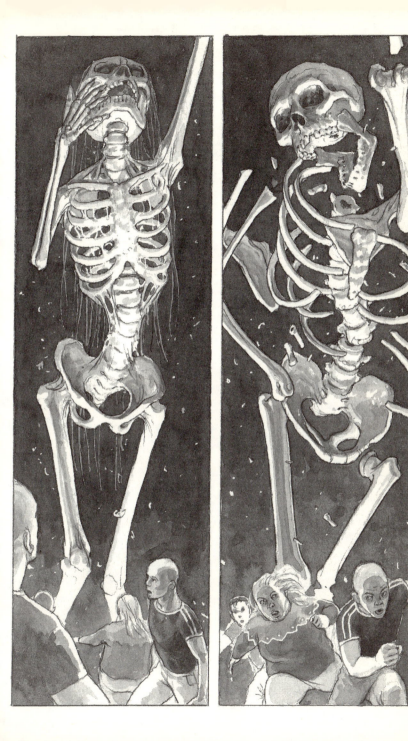

And here is my riddle to help you. This is the first of the elements. The thread of the witch. Use it to colour the sky and make fog appear out of thin air. Goodbye Edric the Wild. And good luck.

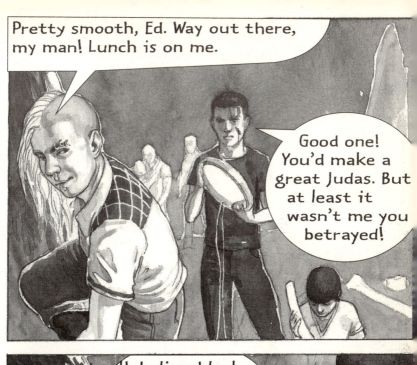

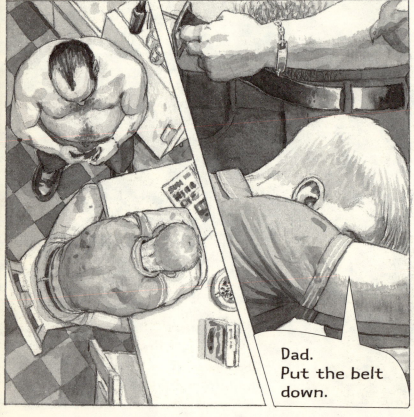

Thread of the witch is
Woven with care,
Fire, earth, water, air;
Hail the sky's long lost daughter,
Air, earth, fire, water;
Life dies, a ghost gives birth,
Water, air, fire, earth;
I stamp and breath a roaring choir,
Earth, air, water, fire:
Bind these elements one by one,
Adding time 'til times are done,
But the sixth, the final prize?
How to meet the enemy's eyes?
Stronger than the singing sword,
This shall have them overawed.